X2

W9-AHG-996

SCAREDY DOG

BY Jane Resh Thomas

ILLUSTRATED BY Marilyn Mets

Hyperion Books for Children
New York

Printed in the United States of America.

First Edition
1 3 5 7 9 10 8 6 4 2

The artwork for each picture is prepared using ink and wash.
This book is set in 20-point Berkeley Book.

Library of Congress Cataloging-in-Publication Data.
Thomas, Jane Resh.
    Scaredy dog / Jane Resh Thomas. — 1st ed.
       p.   cm.
    Summary: With patience and love, a young girl helps the dog she has chosen from the Humane Society grow from a frightened puppy into a happy pet.
     ISBN 0-7868-0278-2 (trade) — ISBN 0-7868-1148-X (pbk.)
     [1. Dogs—Fiction. 2. Animals—Treatment—Fiction.] I. Title.
PZ7.T36695Sc   1996   95-49312
[Fic]—dc20

CONTENTS

·1·
FIRST MEETING

The Humane Society had
fifty-seven dogs, and most of
them were barking. The rest
whined and begged for attention,
their tongues hanging out and
their tails wagging. Choose me!
Take me home with you!

All except the gray one with the
white legs and ruff. He lay curled
up in the back corner of his

kennel, on guard and watching. Erin went inside the cage. The dog froze. Erin put her hand on his head. He trembled and watched her, but still he didn't move. She touched his chest. His heart raced too fast for her to count the beats.

Erin looked into his coffee-colored eyes, and he looked back, unblinking and watching her every move. "I pick him."

"Are you sure?" Mom asked. "He isn't very friendly."

"The rest of them would go off with just anybody. Not him. He's the dog for me."

"I hope you're patient," said the

clerk while Mom and Erin paid the fee. "Two people already have taken him home and brought him back."

"Patient?" Mom's voice sounded tight. "He's nearly six months old. I thought he would be trained."

"A woman kept him and thirty-five other dogs in her house. They were starving when we found them. All but five died." The clerk looked at Erin. "He's a little wild. What he needs is kindness."

"I have plenty of that," said Erin.

·2·
GOING HOME

The noise of the car engine startled the dog so much that he gouged Erin's legs with his claws. Though she held him in her lap, he trembled all the way home.

When she opened the car door, he leaped out, raced across the yard, and hid between the corner of the fence and the oak tree.

Erin dragged him out. She

pulled him and pushed him into the house.

"What will you name him?" asked Mom.

"Mac."

"Scaredy Dog would fit better."

"Mac will fit him when he knows he belongs with me."

Erin held Mac tight. He let her rub his back and stroke his ears, but his eyes were on her, and his

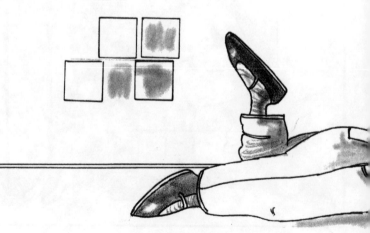

tail didn't wag. The instant she relaxed her grip, he raced around the corner, down the hall, and into the bathroom. He huddled there, between the sink and the tub.

Erin coaxed him. "Come on, boy. I won't hurt you."

Mac watched with eyes so wide Erin could see the whites. He wouldn't budge.

At suppertime, Erin pushed him and pulled him into the kitchen. She offered him a bite of her hamburger, fixed just the way she liked it. Mac wiggled his black gumdrop nose and turned away.

Erin offered him water in his new red bowl. He wouldn't drink it. The minute Erin turned her back, Mac raced into the bathroom and hid behind the sink again.

When Erin did her homework that night, she put Mac's new red collar on him and hooked his

leash around her ankle. But she also put his soft mattress of cedar shavings between the bathroom sink and the tub so he could hide in comfort.

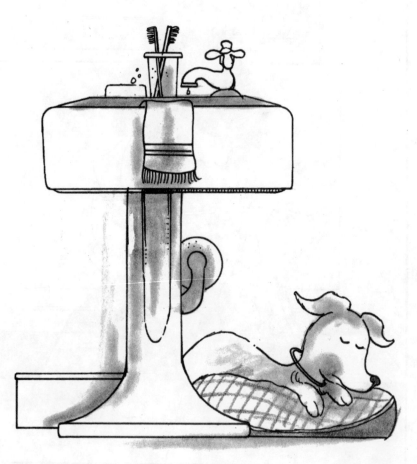

"Taming Mac may be harder than you thought," said Mom.

"The man at the animal shelter said he would need patience," said Erin. "I can give him that."

·3·
MAC LEARNS MANNERS

The next day, Erin took Mac
walking. First he hung back, then
he lunged against the leash so
hard he choked.

"Hi, Mr. Milo," Erin said to her neighbor. "How do you like Mac?"

Mr. Milo looked him over. "What's his breed?"

"Mostly mutt, my mom says."

Mac wound the leash around Erin's legs, trying to hide.

"Not very brave," said Mr. Milo.

"He's had a hard life," said Erin. "Until now."

A car passed them. Mac whirled toward the noise, ready to defend himself.

A bus went by. A truck backfired. Mac nearly fell over from fear.

A Chihuahua trotted past with a tiny growl in its tiny throat. Mac slunk behind a mailbox and made himself small.

He sniffed at the tree on the curb. He inspected the bushes by the door. But he didn't go. He

waited till Erin took him into the house. Then he lifted his leg by the coffee table and peed on Mom's Oriental rug.

"I don't know whether we're patient enough to keep him," said Mom.

"Summer vacation starts next week," Erin said. "I'll take him out every hour."

Soon Mac had tried the bushes by the door, the lamppost, and the mailbox. Erin praised him and petted him every time. Then he discovered the big maple tree at the corner. Whenever he passed, he circled it slowly, sniffing and

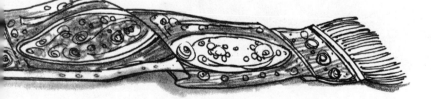

snuffing every new scent as eagerly as if he were reading letters from friends. Finally he left a message of his own. The tree became his favorite spot, the place he went for news of the world. He gave up Mom's Oriental rug.

"He's doing better, thanks to you," said Mom.

"What he needs is friends," said Erin. "And I can be a friend."

·4·
MAC MEETS THE NEIGHBORS

Soon Erin took Mac to meet his other neighbors on the street.

Lana, Mr. Milo's Afghan, looked like a tall movie star wearing pajamas. When she pranced up to Mac with her blond hair flowing, he hid behind Erin again. Lana pushed her head between Erin's knees and licked

Mac's nose. He came out in slow
motion, as if he were planning to
steal something. Lana sniffed him
everywhere. Mac sniffed back.
Lana knelt down on her elbows,
wanting to play. Mac knelt down,
too.

The Sullivans bought a yellow
Labrador puppy and named her
Tanner. When she arrived,
Tanner was the size of Erin's

foot—too small to climb the
steps and so awkward that she
sometimes tripped over her own
big paws. The first time Mac met
her, he ran circles around her,
sometimes knocking her down.
Then he lay panting on his side

and let Tanner climb him as if he were a hill. He drew the line, though, when she bit his nose with her needle teeth. He yelped and leaped away as tiny rubies of blood beaded on his nose. But he didn't bite.

Erin took Mac to the house down the block where Etienne, the big poodle, lived. Etienne

looked like a walking rug. Nearly
every afternoon, he leaped over
his fence and galloped around
town. Now he poked his nose
between the pickets of the fence
and whined and wagged his tail.
Mac gave the poodle's nose a big
wet lick. Etienne jumped the
fence and followed Mac home. In

her own backyard, Erin
unsnapped Mac's leash and let
him go. First Etienne chased
Mac. Then Mac chased Etienne
until they both fell down panting.
After that, whenever Etienne
escaped, he sat on Erin's porch
whining for Mac to come out and
play. Even in the bathroom, Mac

could hear the invitation. He perked up his ears and whined until Erin let him out. The two dogs raced back and forth across the yards in a blur of black and gray and white.

"I suppose I ought to put him on a chain," said Ms. Delton, who lived with Etienne. "But when he disappears, at least I know where to find him."

Now Mac had three friends. Still he hid in Erin's bathroom. He ate only when he thought nobody was looking, sneaking one bite at a time and eating it behind the sink.

Erin kept Mac with her, even

though he would rather be hiding. One day, she lay on the floor, eating grapes and reading, with the leash wrapped around her arm. Mac crept closer and closer until he was snuggled next to her leg. Erin slowly reached down and stroked his belly. Mac

licked her hand. That night, when the lights were out, he climbed up on her bed and licked her neck as if she were made of candy.

"He likes dogs better than people," said Mom.

"But he's getting braver every day. What he needs is love," said Erin, "and I have plenty of that."

·5·
MAC THE FIERCE

A few weeks later, while Erin and
Mom ate supper, Mac crept out
of the bathroom, stole under the
table, and lay down with a clunk of
his bones. Erin felt him delicately lay
his head on her foot.

A few minutes later, he stood and
put his chin on her knee. Still hidden
under the tablecloth, he poked his
head out, laid it on her thigh, and

stared at her with his coffee-
colored eyes.

"We shouldn't feed him at the
table," said Mom. "He'll learn bad
habits."

"Just this once," said Erin. "He
took a chance." She cut off a
corner of her pork chop and
offered it with her fingers.

Mac sniffed the front of the
meat. He sniffed each side. He
sniffed underneath. He tasted it

with the very tip of his tongue.
Then, gently, barely touching
Erin's fingers, he took the meat
between his lips and crept back
behind the sink.

That evening, Mac left the
bathroom without being pushed

and pulled, and stealthily explored the house. Erin followed him. Inspecting Mom's office, he found an old piece of toast that had fallen between her computer and the filing cabinet. He ate it.

In Mom's bedroom, Erin watched him check all the bottles on the dressing table.

He looked in Mom's closet and smelled her shoes, one by one.

Next Erin followed Mac to the living room, where he tried each chair. He picked the one by the window, turned around in it three times, and lay down with a sigh. Soon Erin saw his lips vibrate as he snored.

"Would you look at that!" said Mom. "You've cast a spell on him. He's moved into my old velvet chair as if he owned the place. Looks like I'll have to sit somewhere else."

"What he needed was kindness," said Erin.

"And patience," said Mom.

"And friends."

"And love."

"And a bite of pork chop under the tablecloth."

One day, Mac sat in his favorite chair, leaning his elbows on the windowsill. Waiting for Lana or Etienne or Tanner to happen by, he watched the cats pounce and

roll in the grass across the street.

Mr. Burke, the mail carrier,
came up the walk with the
letters. "Woof," Mac said in the
back of his throat. He nearly fell
off the chair in surprise.

Erin's friend Rob rode his bike
up the front sidewalk. "Roofroof!"

Mac said, a little louder.

Rosie threw the evening paper against the front door. "ROWROW ROWROWROW!"

Mac was so proud of himself, he tried it again.

"ROWROWROWROWROW! ROBBERROBBERROBBER!"

Now that he knows how to bark, Mac isn't a scaredy dog anymore. He guards his family against every noise and every squirrel and every leaf that falls. Mac's name fits him, now that he knows he belongs with Erin.